DREAM BELIEVE ACHIEVE™ SERIES

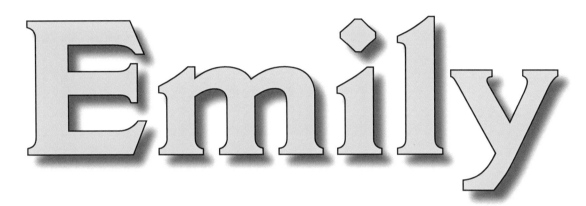

Emily

MARTHA M. SYMINGTON

ILLUSTRATED BY AMANDA M. NOLAN

MARTHA'S MUSINGS INC.

Agio
PUBLISHING HOUSE

Agio
PUBLISHING HOUSE

151 Howe Street, Victoria BC Canada V8V 4K5

With thanks to illustrator Amanda M. Nolan,
editor Jae Desmarais, and Agio Publishing
House's Bruce and Marsha Batchelor.
Author photos by Marlys Symington.

*For rights information and bulk orders, please
contact:* info@agiopublishing.com *or go to*
www.agiopublishing.com

Emily
ISBN 978-1-897435-21-2 (trade paperback)
ISBN 987-1-897435-22-9 (electronic edition)

For more information, we invite you to visit
www.MarthasMusings.com

Printed on acid-free paper that includes no fibre
from endangered forests. Agio Publishing House is a
socially responsible company, measuring success on
a triple-bottom-line basis.

10   9   8   7   6   5   4   3   2   1b

Dedication

To Mom and Dad, for your love and support

Inspired by my niece, Emily

Dear Amanda:

Always follow your dreams!

[signature]

· Dream Believe Achieve ⭐ · · · · · · · · · · · · · · · ·

• A Rare Bug •

Waves slowly rocked the boat as the last scientist climbed aboard. The scientist was troubled as he looked back at the dried-up farmland and lifeless trees.

"Why, just a few weeks ago, people were happily farming here," he thought sadly.

All the families had to move to town. They would never be able to live on their farms again.

"A rare bug has destroyed the soil," the scientist told the families on the shore. "This kind of bug goes away after just three days but the damage they cause lasts forever. Nothing will ever grow here again."

A young farm girl named Emily listened carefully to what the scientist was saying. It sounded hopeless. As she filled a garden pot with farm soil to take with her when they moved, she thought, "I wonder?"

A Dream is Born

One year later

Emily stirred when her alarm clock beeped. For a moment, she was still dreaming of being back on their farm. The sun was shining and the scent of lilacs was in the air. As usual, her yellow lab Sam whimpered to be let out to run in the fields. Her new spotted pony was waiting for her in the barn.

Slowly opening her eyes, Emily looked over at the brightly painted plant pot filled with soil she had secretly taken from their farm when they moved into town. For the past year, she has tried to grow every kind of plant she could find. "One day," she thought, "something will grow!"

Nothing had worked yet, but as her feet hit the floor, Emily yawned her first *Thank You* of the day. She thought, "I have my family, friends and Sam to be thankful for and I get to enter the art contest at school today!" The winner will be picked in a week, the last day of school before summer break. The prize is a huge supply of paints and brushes.

Emily loved to draw and wondered, "What picture will I paint for the contest?"

Emily's stomach growled noisily as she skipped down the hall to the kitchen. Spying her plate of blueberry pancakes topped with whipped cream, she said, "Good Morning."

Her baby sister Katie looked up. Emily and her mom started laughing. Katie had buried her face in whipped cream! She just smiled at them and planted her face back in the whipped cream, making them laugh even harder.

After eating her own stack of yummy pancakes, Emily helped her mom clean up.

Saying "Good-bye" as she ran to catch her school bus, she thought about the art contest again and wondered, "What picture will I paint?"

When her school bus drove by the deserted farmland, as usual, everyone stopped talking. Pressing her nose against the window of the bus, Emily stared at the *No Trespassing* signs and wire fences. She tried to see their old farmhouse but all she could see was dry, cracked earth and huge tumbleweeds.

Closing her eyes for a minute, she thought, "I know *exactly* what picture I will paint for the contest!"

• Art Contest •
The last day of school

The last day of school was finally here! Unable to sit still, Emily wiggled around in her desk chair. The whole class was excited. Mostly because it was the last day of school before summer break. Also, today they pick the winner of the art contest.

Emily dreamed of winning the prize so she could paint a much bigger picture. Her bedroom wall would be perfect. She would paint her winning picture and wake up every morning looking at their old farm and the spotted pony of her dreams.

Their teacher, Miss Thompson, entered the classroom. Emily held her breath and stared at the folded paper in the teacher's hand. "Please, let it be me!" she thought.

Opening the paper, Miss Thompson said, "And the winner is— Emily!"

Jumping for joy, Emily knocked her chair across the room. The whole class started laughing.

Grinning from ear to ear, Emily gathered up her winning picture and new paint supplies. Hurrying to catch her bus, she said, "Now, I have a wall to paint."

• Sharing the Dream •
The first day of summer break

Emily got up early the next morning. It was summer break and she had a plan! She needed to ask her parents and their landlord if she could paint her bedroom wall.

After washing the breakfast dishes and sweeping out the garage, Emily taped her winning picture to the wall facing her bed. The stage was set.

Calling her parents to her room, she told them what she wanted. "Please," she begged, "look at my picture before you say anything!"

When they saw her picture, the look on their faces gave her the answer she wanted.

Okay, two down and one to go....

Their landlord Ovy should be easy to convince. Emily used her recycling money to buy his favorite kind of food: a pizza. Everyone calls him Anchovy Ovy because he loves his pizzas *smothered* in smelly anchovies.

Holding the stinky pizza, she knocked on Ovy's door and thought, "I hope this works!"

When he opened the door, he said, "Why Emily, you've brought my favorite food. Please come in!"

While he ate his stinky pizza, she told him the plan. And, guess what?

He said, "Yes!"

Emily said, "Thank you, Ovy!" and raced home to start painting.

Rolling up her shirt sleeves, Emily took out her new paint and brushes. Humming all her favorite songs, she painted her dream picture on the bedroom wall.

Stepping back to admire her picture, she thought, "It looks exactly as I remember it from living there. Well, not quite, because the spotted pony is new."

"Everyone, close your eyes," Emily said when they entered her bedroom. When she sang out, "Ta da!" they opened their eyes.

"Why, Emily, that's a beautiful picture. It looks exactly like our old farm," her mother said. "I love your new spotted pony too!"

They had so much fun remembering stories about their old farm, that her mom made a picnic and they ate it in Emily's bedroom.

• Dream Blooms •

One week later

Early Saturday morning, Emily ate quickly and hurried to watch her dad doing his weekly radio show.

People called in to talk on the radio about life on their old farms. Emily loved to listen to the stories. They were *always* funny. Since leaving the farm, this was the one time each week that her dad seemed really happy.

As she watched him, she thought, "What if I could paint a *really, really* big picture of our old farm in front of the *No Trespassing* signs and wire fences? That way, everyone would remember happier times when they drove by."

She told her dad about her idea. At first, Emily thought he might say no, but he smiled and said, "Why not?"

He got back on the radio to tell people about Emily's idea.

The phone started ringing. People from all over wanted to give supplies for the giant billboard. Some even offered to help paint it!

When Emily and her family arrived the next morning, they were very surprised. The whole town was there! A huge billboard had been built in front of the wire fences. People were painting pictures of their old farms. There were big picnic hampers filled with food and Fred's ice-cream truck was giving free ice-cream to everyone!

As she stepped out of the truck, the crowd shouted, "Hooray for Emily!"

Smiling, she waved at everyone and skipped over to an empty spot on the billboard to start painting.

As she was putting the last spot on her dream pony, Fanny, an island elder, pointed her cane at a leafy plant Emily had painted and asked, "Where did you see that plant, young lady?"

Laughing, Emily said, "Only in my dreams."

Fanny's eyes sparkled with interest. She said, "It looks *exactly* like a potato plant farmed here over one hundred years ago. Now, it only grows wild in one small area at the other end of the island."

Emily got goosebumps all over and asked, "Where can I find these plants?"

After listening carefully to the directions, she gave Fanny a big hug and said, "Thank you!"

That afternoon, Emily rode her bike to the small area where the potato plants grow. When she saw the plants, she said, "They *do* look exactly like the plants in my painting!"

Carefully, she dug out one of the plants to put in the pot of farm soil in her bedroom.

Before falling asleep that night, she thought about the wonderful day she had. Then she said to her new plant, "Please be alive in the morning!"

• Discovery •
Four weeks later

Emily looked over at her plant. "Four weeks and it hasn't grown at all," she thought. "But at least it's still alive. Nothing else survived more than a day!" She watered it, wishing it would grow.

After finishing her morning chores she took Sam and Ovy's little dog Buddy for a walk down a well-worn path to the beach. Emily loved to look for sea shells and had just spotted a perfect one, when Sam and Buddy started barking.

"I wonder what they found?" she thought.

Scrambling down the rocks, she saw her school friends playing volleyball. Sam and Buddy were running circles around the court. It was one of her favorite games so she joined in.

When Emily got home, she skipped to her room with the new shells she had collected. She would put them around her potato plant. When she saw the plant in the pot, she stopped and just stared.

"Wow, it has new leaves! It grew," Emily thought excitedly. "Now I need to see if it can grow on our farmland. I'll get my friends to help me."

She emailed her friends, and asked, "Interested in an adventure? Want to find out about an exciting discovery? Bring your wagons and planting tools and meet me in the park tomorrow morning at nine o'clock."

• **Planting Adventure** •
The next morning

The next morning, Emily loaded her wagon with supplies and her potted potato plant. She hooked her wagon behind her bike and rode to the park. All her friends were there waiting for her.

She told them about Fanny and the potato that hasn't been farmed for over one hundred years. Pointing at the potted plant, Emily said, "That's the soil from our farm, *after* the bug was there. It's actually growing. If it works on our old farms, we could live there again!"

She then lead them to the place where the potato plants grew. Gathering as many plants as they could fit into their wagons, Emily and her friends hurried to the old farms.

After planting all of the potatoes, Emily told them, "It will take four weeks before we'll know if it worked. Four *very* long weeks."

• Magic! •
Four weeks later

Emily felt a bubble of excitement when she woke up. It was exactly four weeks since the potatoes were planted. This was the day they would find out if it had worked.

After breakfast, she got on her bike and raced to the park to meet her friends. No one said anything, but Emily could see they were as excited as she was.

As soon as they arrived at the old farms, they disappeared behind the billboards. "It worked!" someone shouted.

Soon they were smiling, laughing and hugging each other. Emily could barely speak, it was so beautiful. A sea of green covered the fields. The potato plants had doubled in size. Even the trees and wildflowers had started growing again!

Racing back to town, Emily said, "I'll ask my dad to tell the whole town about this on the radio. Wait until they see it!"

This was a day that everyone would remember, especially Emily.

• Endless Possibilities •

One year later

The sun was shining and the air smelled of lilacs. It was Emily's favorite kind of day. After eating breakfast with her family, she skipped to the barn with Sam. Emily was still amazed that her dreams had come true. Everyone was back living on their farms and the land was more beautiful than ever!

She saddled her pony Patch. No one could explain how Betsy, an old brown workhorse, had given birth to a *spotted* pony. Especially one that looked *exactly* like the one in Emily's painting and not *one bit* like old Betsy!

Galloping through the fields, she looked back at the house and waved to Katie who was happily swinging from the tire in their old tree.

Wondering what picture she would draw next, Emily thought, "The possibilities are *endless*!"

Explore the second book in the *Dream Believe Achieve*™ series,

GLOBAL HEART WARMING

Fly along in Dream Star's fun adventure to discover a way
to send an important message *every* human on Earth will understand.
For more information, visit www.MarthasMusings.com.

PAY IT FORWARD

A movie called *Pay it Forward* held an inspirational message for me. In the spirit of *paying it forward*, for each *Dream Believe Achieve*™ book, ten percent (10%) of the net profits will be donated to one of five charities I value and applaud. At my niece Emily's request, donations from the sale of *Emily: Dream Believe Achieve* books will be donated to *Oprah's Angel Network* (www.oprahsangelnetwork.org).

Other charities supported are:
Canadian Children's Wish Foundation (www.childrenswish.ca)
Coady International Institute (www.coady.stfx.ca)
UNICEF (www.unicef.org)
World Vision (www.worldvision.org)

After each book is published, you will be able to see how much has been donated – just log on to my website (www.MarthasMusings.com) and go to the *Charities* section. Then click on the book of your choice to see the progress, and make your own donation!

ABOUT THE AUTHOR

MARTHA M. SYMINGTON

Martha Symington lives on Vancouver Island with her husband Doug and their 11-year-old yellow lab, Sam. When she isn't writing, editing or reading books, Martha spends hours in the garden contemplating the next story.

A graduate of St. Francis Xavier University, Martha enjoyed a successful 20-year career in human resources management before retiring to take on new challenges. She decided on writing children's books and maybe some other stuff… as yet to be developed. Thus Martha's Musings Inc. was born.

Martha's goal is to give every child what Martha herself experienced with *The Wonderful World of Disney* and *Dr. Seuss*. These book series provided laughter, excitement and the thrill of possibilities. From that ideal, the *Dream Believe Achieve*™ series emerged.

Martha has 14 nieces and nephews and says her series will have at least 14 books in it!

Printed in the United States
140061LV00001B